MARCH IS FOR MILES

MOUNTAIN MEN OF MUSTANG MOUNTAIN

DYLANN CRUSH

EVE LONDON

To the Match of the Month Patrons, especially...

Jackie Ziegler

Thank you so much for your support. We couldn't do what we love without you!

Dear Reader,

Thanks for picking up a copy of March is for Miles, book three in the Mountain Men of Mustang Mountain series! We can't wait for you to meet Miles and Kinley. If you love their story and want to learn more about Mustang Mountain, sign up for our newsletter here: http://subscribepage.io/MatchOfTheMonth.

XOXO,
Dylann & Eve

March is for Miles

She's running from her past. He'll do anything to be her future.

Kinley

When I find my fiancé getting busy with my maid of honor fifteen minutes before I'm supposed to walk down the aisle, it's time to face the truth.

I don't think, I just run… right into the front seat of a stranger's truck.

He's bearded and brawny and makes my heart race in a way my ex never did.

With nowhere to go, and no one I can depend on, it would be so tempting to let the mountain man take care of me… if only for a day or two.

Miles

She's gorgeous with those big brown eyes and curves that won't quit. But that bruise on her cheek tells me there's more to this runaway bride's story than she's letting on.

All I want to do is wrap her in my arms and keep her safe. Kinley deserves to be loved for the sweet, precious woman she is, and I'm desperate to be the man she can count on.

Until the past catches up to us... and one mistake might put an end to my dreams of a life together.

Welcome to Mustang Mountain where love runs as wild as the free-spirited horses who roam the hillsides. Framed by rivers, lakes, and breathtaking mountains, it's also the place the Mountain Men of Mustang Mountain call home. They might be rugged and reclusive, but they'll risk their hearts for the curvy girls they love.

DRIVING through the middle of downtown Mustang Mountain wasn't how I liked to spend my Friday nights. But Jackson and Emma had invited me out to dinner to celebrate their engagement, so I'd put on a clean pair of jeans and my best button-down shirt. I hadn't quite forgiven my best friend for taking up with my little sister, but a man could only hold a grudge for so long, especially if there was an expensive dinner involved. It was time to make up, and I couldn't think of a better way to do it than over elk medallions and a stiff pour of bourbon. All on Jackson's dime, of course.

I was just about at the corner where the ice cream shop sat. Seemed pretty crowded for such a cold night. Back where I grew up in San Diego, when temps dipped into the fifties, people put on parkas and went out for hot chocolate. They never would have thought about treating themselves to ice cream. I chuckled to myself. That was one of the things I loved about living in Montana. The folks around Mustang Mountain never let the cold prevent them from doing anything.

I squinted as a family stepped out of the shop. Even from twenty yards away, I recognized Ford. He had one hand wrapped around a waffle cone, and the other behind the woman at his side. Thank fuck he'd come to his senses and got his head out of his ass when it came to Luna. The whole town could tell the two of them belonged together. Poor fucker was the last one to realize it.

Based on the lack of space between them, his efforts had paid off. It had taken the better part of a week to figure out who'd gone after Luna, then a few more days for him to find that ring her douchebag ex had stolen and pawned. My pulse spiked just thinking about it. With that dick behind bars, Ford would never have to worry about Luna's safety again.

I wondered if he'd popped the question yet. It was inevitable. First, Jackson and Emma. Now, Ford and Luna. Ruby's plan to get the Mustang Mountain Riders matched up might not be going exactly like she imagined, but love was in the air. I could smell it like the promise of a late winter storm hovering over the mountains. All the guys were betting on who she'd set her sights on next. She'd better not have any ideas about making me part of her bullshit plan.

My life was perfect exactly like it was. I ran a successful software business that let me set my own hours, pick my own clients, and work wherever I wanted. Being a one-man operation meant I didn't have to rely on anyone, and that's how I wanted it. I'd built my cabin on Mustang Mountain with my own hands and didn't have to answer to anyone about anything. Yeah, I loved my life. Though, sometimes I wondered what it would be like to have someone to share it with.

The light changed to green. Enough with the sappy introspection. I lifted my foot from the brake and was about to step on the gas when a flurry of white appeared in my peripheral vision.

The passenger-side door of my truck opened and a huge ball of lace jumped into the cab. "Go, go, go!"

"What the hell do you think you're doing?" I tightened my grip on the steering wheel. There was no reason for me to feel threatened by the woman underneath the layers and layers of white, but shit like this didn't happen in Mustang Mountain.

A face appeared in the middle of the big white bundle. Her cheek sported an angry red mark and appeared to be swelling by the second. Big brown eyes pleaded with me. "I've got to get out of here. Please."

I'd never seen her before in my life, but the fear in her eyes made a permanent imprint, and I knew I'd never forget it as long as I lived. She looked like a wounded animal who'd been fighting for its life, but knew the end was near. The need to protect her surged within me. My foot hit the gas just as a dark-haired guy in a tux reached for the door handle.

The woman yelled as I accelerated. She grabbed onto my arm, her chest heaving hard underneath the layers of white fabric. I took the road out of town to put some distance between the two of us and whoever was after her. When I felt like we'd gone far enough, I pulled over to the side of the road.

I glanced over at her. Black lines streaked her cheeks. Her hair had come loose, and soft, dark waves framed her face. She met my gaze for the briefest moment, her brown eyes full of apprehension. Fuck, she was beautiful. The cage I'd built around my heart rattled.

Keeping my tone low and soft, I turned toward her and said, "I need to ask you something."

"What's that?" Her voice came out shaky and on the verge of tears.

"Who the hell are you?"

"I'm sorry. You must think I'm a lunatic." She swiped the back of her hand across her cheeks, smearing her makeup even more.

I reached over to grab a pack of tissues from the glove box. My gut twisted as she flinched. Whoever she was, she was scared. "I'm just going to get you a tissue."

Even in the dim light of the truck cab, I could see her white-knuckled grip on the door handle. Like she was ready to jump out of the truck and run if she felt threatened. But it was March in the mountains and that strapless cloud of white fabric would do nothing to protect her against the elements.

"You want to tell me what happened?" She reminded me of an injured doe I'd come across last spring. It had stumbled into a hole and twisted its leg.

The wary way the woman studied me mimicked the same serious consideration the doe had given me. If I wanted any information, I'd have to take a slow and soft approach.

"Not really. Is there a bus station or somewhere you can take me? I need to get out of town right away." She took the small pack of tissues I handed her, then pressed herself against the door of the truck while she wiped her tears away.

"You're not from around here, are you?" I already knew the answer to that. Anyone familiar with the area would know the only form of public transportation around these parts involved sticking out a thumb on the side of the road. It was tricky to find a ride in the summer, much less this time of year.

"I live in Coeur d'Alene, and I'm just in town for a wedding."

"Would that be your wedding?" I prompted.

"Yes. My fiance's family is from around here so they wanted to have the wedding in Mustang Mountain. I guess he's my ex fiance now. I can't go back there." Her lower lip trembled. "Can you take me somewhere I can call a rideshare or a cab? Somewhere he can't find me?"

My fingers curled into fists. Whoever she was running from needed to be taught a lesson on how to treat a woman. But first, I had to get the runaway bride somewhere safe. "We don't have cabs or ride shares, but I'd be happy to take you wherever you want to go."

Her shoulders hunched over and she covered her

face with her hands. "That's just it. I don't have anywhere to go."

I wanted to offer her comfort but was afraid if I touched her she'd run and I'd end up chasing her down the highway. Some of the other guys in the MC had experience helping victims of domestic abuse. Like my buddy Jensen. His friend ran a shelter for women and children a few towns over. If I could convince this woman to let me contact them, they'd know what to do.

"There's a place outside of town where you can stay for a few days until you decide what to do. I can give them a call and figure out a place to meet up so they can take you over there if you want."

"What kind of place?"

"It's a shelter. I know the woman who runs it, and I'm sure she'll be better prepared to help you with whatever you need." The fear in her eyes slayed me. Whoever had her running deserved a special place in hell. There was a good chance I'd be able to find him if I wanted to after I made sure she was safe. I'd just look for a huge dick in a tux. Shouldn't be too difficult in a town where most men wore jeans and flannel. "What do you think? Should I give them a call?"

"Okay." She bit down on her lower lip as she lifted her head and met my gaze. "Thank you."

"No need to thank me. I'm Miles." Relieved that we had a plan, I instinctively offered my hand, but immediately regretted it. The last thing this woman needed was to be touched by a man right now.

"I'm Kinley." She slid her palm against mine. Tiny pulses of awareness skittered up my arm.

I broke contact. It didn't matter how my body reacted to the gorgeous woman in the wedding gown. I had one immediate goal: get her to someone who could help her with whatever she was going through. I'd knew myself well enough to be sure I wasn't the man for the job.

I WRAPPED my arms around my waist while he made the call. Shame at letting myself get into a situation like this threatened to strangle me. It was all my fault. I was the one who put up with Doug for far too long. I should have walked out on him the first time he hurt me. Or the second or the third or... I'd lost count of how many times he'd lifted his hand to me in anger.

Once he cooled off, he'd always beg and plead for me not to leave him. He was sorry... he'd try harder... he'd finally go get the help he needed. He could be so sweet when he wasn't under the influence of whatever drugs he was taking.

That's why I stayed. All I wanted was to reconnect with the man I'd fallen in love with back in high school. I should have realized years ago that the only place that man existed anymore was in my memories of the past.

Doug had mastered the art of sweet talk and making promises he never intended to keep. Somehow he sucked me back in time and time again until I actually started to believe that he was right, and I was the one to blame for him losing control.

I snuck a glance at the man sitting behind the wheel while we waited for someone to pick up the other end of the line. I'd had one hand on the door handle since the moment I'd realized I'd jumped into the front seat of a brawny mountain man's truck. Why couldn't I have picked an SUV with a woman behind the wheel? I suppose I wasn't thinking about the consequences when I ran into traffic with Doug hot on my heels and dove into the first vehicle I reached.

Miles hadn't given me any reason to worry. He'd been nothing but kind since I'd forced myself on him. It's not like I'd given him much of a choice. If Doug had caught me before I got away... I didn't want to think about the consequences. Standing up to him in the privacy of our own home was one thing. Embarrassing him by walking out of our wedding in front of his friends and family could have had serious results.

Thinking about him made my pulse spike. I reminded myself I was safe. At least safer than I'd been a half hour ago. Safer than I'd been most of my adult life.

Finally, a recorded woman's voice came on the line with instructions to dial 9-1-1 if it was an emergency or to leave a message and someone would return the call as soon as they could. Miles cleared his throat and left a message. Then he hung up and glanced over.

His eyes softened at the edges. "I don't want to

head that way unless they know we're coming. Do you want me to take you somewhere while we wait to hear back?"

Tears stung the back of my throat. I couldn't ask this man to do more than he already had. But I had nowhere to go. No family. No friends.

"Or I could take you to the police stat—"

"No police."

Miles angled his body to face me. "What kind of trouble are you in, Kinley?"

I looked out the window at the snow-covered landscape. We were on the side of a stretch of road that cut through the mountains. There was nowhere to go.

I tried to swallow around the huge lump forming in my throat. "The kind you don't want any part of. I'm sorry. I never should have pulled you into this. If you could just drop me off somewhere in town, I'll figure things out."

"There's one other place I can take you."

At that point, he could have offered to drive me straight to the devil's front door and I would have taken him up on it. Nothing would be worse than crawling back to Doug and having to face his wrath. "Yes, please."

"You don't even know where it is yet." He shifted the truck into gear and made a U-turn.

"As long as you're not taking me back to that church, I don't care where it is." I'd always wondered when I'd finally know when I'd had enough. I guess finding my fiancé completely wasted and banging my maid of honor fifteen minutes before I was supposed to walk down the aisle was my limit.

"Is there anyone you can call? A friend? Family member?"

I shook my head. There was no one left. Doug ran off all of my friends, and I'd lost my dad to a car crash when I was five and my mom to cancer a few years ago. That's why I'd been so reluctant to try to leave.

"The shelter ought to call back in a little bit. Until then, we can head up the mountain to my place."

Even though I had no reason to doubt his intentions, I tensed. It's not like I could hide out in town and hope no one from the wedding would recognize me. Not in my frothy, lacy, getaway gown. If I wanted to be on my own, I'd need to start taking chances.

"That would be... great," I forced out.

"I don't know where else to take you. My sister lives in a cabin just up the hill. She's out to dinner right now with her fiance, but I'll ask her to stop by on the way home if that will make you feel more comfortable."

He kept casting nervous glances my way, like he was worried I'd hop out of the truck and try my luck racing across the snow-covered hills. I could have told him not to worry about that. I'd tried it once and didn't get very far before I had to turn back. Even though I would have gladly chosen freezing to death over spending another night under the same roof as Doug, my sense of self-preservation won.

"I can promise you this,"—his eyes met mine across the darkness of the truck cab—"whoever did that to you will never lay a hand on you again. Not while I'm around."

Resting my forehead against the window, I hoped with all my heart I could believe him.

WE PULLED up in front of my cabin, and I tried to see it through Kinley's eyes. She hadn't said anything on the drive up the mountain, not even when a couple of deer darted across the road and I had to slam on the brakes. If I were in her shoes right now, I'd be looking for a stiff pour of whiskey and somewhere to pass out for a few hours. I might not be able to fix whatever issue she'd left at the bottom of the mountain, but I could at least offer her that.

"It's bigger than it looks inside," I told her. I was proud of my cabin. It might lack the craftsmanship of Jackson's, but it was perfect for me, and it had been my refuge for the past few years. Mine, and mine alone. Kinley would be the first woman besides my sister to ever step across the threshold.

"It looks really nice." Her voice came out soft and small. Now that we were about to walk into my place together, I wondered if she was having second thoughts.

"Let me help you down." I held out a hand to help her out of the truck. She had her dress all bunched up in her arms. There was no way she'd make it up the walk to the front door in that thing, especially when I couldn't tell what kind of shoes she had on underneath.

I shrugged off my coat and rested it over her bare shoulders.

"You don't have to do that." Even with red-rimmed eyes, she was beautiful.

"Can you make it up to the door, or should I carry you?"

She held tight to my elbow. "I can make it. It's not like I need to be careful of my dress anymore."

We made it inside, and I stomped my feet on the big rug in the entryway before I pulled off my boots. "The den and kitchen are to your left. I'll get you something to change into so you can get out of that dress."

She waited in the foyer while I rushed to my bedroom and rummaged through my drawers. I returned with a pair of sweats that would swim on her and a well-worn sweatshirt.

"I'm so sorry to be such a pain." She took the clothes I held out. "I'll get out of here as soon as I can."

"Don't worry about it. People around here look out for each other. I'm not doing anything someone else wouldn't have done if you'd jumped into their front seat." I tried to keep the tone light. Now that we were back at my place—alone—I didn't want to scare her. She had nothing to fear from me.

"Do you mind if I change?"

"Second door on your right down the hall. I'll make a pot of coffee and a fire to warm you up." I waited until I heard the bathroom door close behind her, then headed to the kitchen to get that coffee started. While she was changing, I fired off a text to Jackson to let him know I wouldn't make it to dinner. I also asked him to stop by with Emma on the way home. Kinley would be safe here with me, but she'd probably be more comfortable at the shelter or staying with the two of them. After what she'd been through, I didn't want her to feel threatened.

She didn't make a sound when she entered the kitchen on bare feet, so when I turned around and saw her standing in the door, my heartbeat spiked. She'd taken her hair down, and it fell around her shoulders in long, dark waves. My sweats hung on her hips and pooled at her feet. Free from that huge dress, I could appreciate her curves. She was the most gorgeous woman I'd ever seen.

"Can I get you some coffee?" I tamped down the inferno of attraction blazing inside. The very last thing this woman needed was me acting like a sex-starved idiot around her.

"I'd like that." The nervous glances she cast my way practically begged me to wrap her in my arms and protect her.

The feeling didn't catch me off guard, but the

intensity did. I'd always been protective of those who needed it, and this woman definitely needed someone in her corner. I filled a mug and slid it across the counter to her.

"Do you need cream or sugar or a nip of something stronger to settle your nerves?"

Her eyebrows arched. "Just cream and sugar if you have it."

I sent a silent thanks to Emma for insisting I keep coffee creamer in my fridge for the very rare occasion when she stopped over.

Kinley poured a bit into her mug, then handed it back to me. Our fingers brushed as I took it from her. Heat radiated up my arm. What the fuck was wrong with me?

"How about some ice for that cheek?" The area under her eye had started to turn a mottled bluish-purplish color. By tomorrow, she'd probably have a black eye.

She reached up and rubbed her fingers over her cheek. "It's not as bad as it looks."

My guess was this wasn't the first time she'd dealt with a few bruises. The thought of anyone hurting her made me want to punch something... or better yet... the asshole who'd hurt her.

"You want to sit in front of the fire?" I gestured to the den where I had a decent fire going.

She took a seat in the overstuffed leather chair, so I sat down on the sofa. I'd let her drive the conversation. My goal was to make sure she was comfortable until I could get her to someone with more experience in this type of thing. If it were up to me, I'd have her lock herself in my cabin while I went back to town to beat the fuck out of the piece of shit who'd hit her.

"Thanks for... everything." She let out a heavy sigh. "I'm sorry for inconveniencing you."

I leaned forward. "You're not an inconvenience. You want to tell me what happened? If you'd rather not, I understand."

She bit down on her bottom lip and glanced at the fire. "I suppose if I want to end the cycle and break free, I need to start talking about it."

"I can be a good listener if you want one."

"If I'm being honest, I don't know what I want right now."

I took a sip of my coffee to keep myself from interrupting.

She kept her gaze locked on the fire while she started to talk. "Doug and I met in high school. He was two years older than me. You know the type, right? Captain of the football team, most popular guy in school. I couldn't believe he was interested in me."

I almost choked on my sip of coffee. She had no idea how gorgeous she was.

"I was flattered. It was just me and my mom at home, and she worked two jobs to keep food on the table. Doug came from the other side of the tracks, if you know what I mean. He started taking me places I only dreamed about. Fancy dinners, skiing vacations with his family... it was great for a while." Her big brown eyes focused on me briefly before she looked down at her hands. "Until it wasn't."

"You don't have to go on if you don't want to."

Her shoulders rolled. "I'll have to tell someone to get into the shelter. Maybe it will be easier if I practice on you."

I was more than willing to listen, even if it meant suppressing my rage. "Go on then, Kinley. Tonight marks the end of that part of your life. Get it out and get it over."

She nodded and drew in a shaky breath. "He stayed in town for college, so we were always together. Once I graduated from high school, he moved me into his apartment. His world kept growing, but mine was shrinking. He didn't want me hanging out with my friends anymore. Barely wanted me going to visit my own mother. If I questioned him on anything, he turned it around and accused me of not believing in him."

What a motherfucker. I'd heard similar stories from some of the women my other MC brothers had helped in the past.

"The first time he hit me was when I burned a pot of spaghetti sauce. He said the only thing I was good for was cooking, cleaning and um,"—she lifted a shoulder, and her lower lip trembled as she sucked in a deep breath—"I guess I'll call it bedroom stuff. He told me I'd better figure out how to become an expert in all three or he wouldn't have any use for me."

My stomach hitched into a tight knot as I forced

myself not to reach for her. Seeing the pain in her eyes had me two seconds away from heading back down the mountain. "You don't have to keep going."

"I believed him for so long." Her chin tipped up, and a glimmer of defiance flashed in her eyes. "I mean, he was the college graduate. I'd barely made it through high school."

I wanted to comfort her, but I didn't know how. So I just sat there and let her get her story out of her system, hoping it was the right thing to do.

"Things got worse after that. He started hanging out with some guys at his new job, and they spent a lot of time entertaining clients. That meant lots of partying, and he got hooked on drugs. I left him then, but he always came after me, promising he'd clean up his act, saying he couldn't live without me." Her fingers swiped away a stray tear. "I always took him back."

My phone rang, interrupting the moment. I glanced at the screen, then looked over at Kinley. "It's my contact at the shelter."

She nodded as I answered. I gave a few details about the situation and the woman on the other end of the line said she'd call back in a few minutes with a time and location where we could meet up with one of their contacts. When I hung up, I filled Kinley in on the details. She tugged a tissue free from a box on the side table and dabbed at her eyes.

"Are you okay with all of this?" I asked. She'd been through so much.

"I'm sure I will be, though right now all I want to

do is close my eyes and sleep for the next week, or so at least. Everything's happening so fast." We stood at the same time.

The scent of her perfume drifted up to my nose. She smelled like the flowers in the valley in the summer. My fingers itched to pull her close while I promised to protect her. Even though we'd just met, I wasn't ready to let her go.

"If you'd rather..." I stopped myself from saying any more. It was a ridiculous idea. She belonged with people who could help her out of her situation.

"If I'd rather what?" Big doe eyes stared up at me.

Suddenly nervous as hell, I tried to make myself sound nonchalant. "I was just thinking it's getting kind of late. If you'd rather sleep in the guest room tonight, I can take you wherever you need to go tomorrow. But I don't want you to be uncomfortable. I'm more than happy to drive you back down the mountain tonight. Whatever you want."

Her lips parted like she was about to say something. I could sense her reluctance hovering between us. Then she put her hand on my arm. "I feel safe here, Miles. If you're sure it's not too much trouble, I'd like to stay with you, at least until tomorrow."

THE MORE TIME I spent around the tall, broad-shouldered mountain man, the more comfortable I felt. For the first time in as long as I could remember, I wasn't afraid. Logically, I should be. We were at the top of a mountain, just the two of us. No one would be able to hear me if I screamed. If he tried to force himself on me, there would be no one to help. But deep in my heart, I somehow knew he'd never try to hurt me.

I could see it in his eyes. He was the kind of man I wished I'd found years ago. The kind of man I didn't believe existed. And I'd just spent the night in his guest room. I was wearing his clothes, curling up under his covers, and trying to convince myself the feelings burning their way through me were the result of him coming to my rescue. There couldn't be anything more to them.

It was natural to feel something toward a man who'd saved me. I was grateful. That was all. I'd just left an emotionally and physically abusive relationship. My heart and mind couldn't be trusted to make sound decisions. I needed time and space before I could even consider letting another man touch me. But there was something about Miles that made me want to forget about being rational.

Whatever I was feeling didn't matter. He'd take me down the mountain later on today and finally be free of me and the drama that followed me around like a damn black cloud. I tossed the covers back and got out of bed. It was time to start a new chapter in my life.

The scent of strong coffee beckoned, so I crept down the hall. Hushed voices came from the kitchen.

"What are you going to do with her?" a woman asked.

"I don't know. Is it wrong that I want to keep her here and protect her?" Miles asked. My chest squeezed tight at the question. I couldn't let him get involved. If Doug had any idea where I was, he'd come after me. There was no way I'd put Miles or his family at risk.

"Good morning." I wrapped my arms around my waist and stepped into the kitchen. A woman and man sat at the table across from Miles. For a split second, I wondered if he'd called them to come take me away.

Miles got up and moved to the counter to pour me a cup of coffee. "I hope we didn't wake you."

"Not at all." I waited while he added creamer to my mug.

"This is my sister Emma and my best friend Jackson. They also happen to be engaged." He handed me the mug of coffee and pulled a chair away from the table. "I asked them to stop by on their way home last night, but you were asleep by the time they got here. Do you want to join us?"

The three of them were fully dressed, and I felt totally out of place in the sweats and sweatshirt Miles gave me. "Um, sure."

Emma handed me a bag. "I know what it's like to be stranded without clothes. You're welcome to see if any of these fit."

"Thank you." I shot a quick look at Miles. The encouraging smile he gave me soothed my nerves. He and his sister must be close if he'd called her.

"Miles was filling us in on what happened last night. Sounds like you've been through quite a bit. Is there anything we can do to help?" Jackson put his arm around Emma while he talked. The two of them looked so natural together. They were what an engaged couple should look like. Things between me and Doug had never been so easy, though I yearned for that kind of relationship.

"I was just telling Jackson about your place in Coeur d'Alene. If you want me to take you to grab your things, I can call a few guys to go with us." Miles nodded toward Jackson. "We're part of a MC and have plenty of muscle who'd be willing to back us up."

"What's a MC?" I asked.

"A motorcycle club," Emma answered. "These guys are part of the Mustang Mountain Riders and actually do a lot of good deeds around town as part of the club."

The only motorcycle gangs I'd seen were the rough and rowdy ones on TV. "How can you ride a motorcycle up and down this mountain?"

Miles chuckled. "It's a seasonal thing. The motorcycles, I mean."

The coffee slid down my throat into an empty stomach. I hadn't had anything to eat since lunch the day before. Lunch Doug's mom had catered in for me and the rest of the wedding party. Even though I couldn't care less, I wondered what they were all doing now... what kind of sob story Doug might be giving them about how I'd run away for no reason and broken his heart.

Jackson's phone pinged with an alert. He glanced down and his brow creased. "We might have a bit of an issue."

"What's up?" Miles put his hand over mine where it rested on the table.

That small gesture of reassurance was exactly what I needed.

"Looks like Kinley's been reported as a missing person." Jackson held his phone up so we could see the screen.

My cheeks heated. Doug would do anything to save face. He probably told the wedding guests I'd had a mental breakdown.

"I'll call the sheriff's office and explain the situation." Miles pulled his hand away to pick up his phone.

"I need to talk to him," I said. "In person. That's the only way to get him to leave me alone."

"Are you sure?" Miles leaned forward, the area around his eyes creased with concern. "You don't have to do that, Kinley."

I shifted my gaze to meet his. "Yes, I do, and I need to grab a few things I left behind. It's a lot to ask, but would you be willing to go with me?"

"Of course." He set down his phone and grabbed my hands in both of his. "I'd never let you face him alone."

FIVE HOURS LATER, I knocked on the front door of the townhouse I'd shared with Doug. He'd never even given me a key. All the red flags were so obvious now. I couldn't believe I hadn't seen them sooner.

He answered the door in a pair of sweats and a wife beater tee. The irony wasn't lost on me.

"Look who came crawling back." Doug stepped aside and gestured for me to come in. "You've got a lot of explaining to do, Kinley."

"She's not crawling back, asshole. Kinley has something to say to you, and I'm here to make sure you listen." Miles stepped forward, shielding me with his body.

I would have given just about anything to capture a picture of Doug's reaction. In all the time we'd been together, I'd never seen anyone talk to him like that.

"What did you want to say?" Miles turned to face

me, his voice soft, his expression full of patience—quite a change from the look he'd just given my ex.

I cleared my throat. As much as I wanted to put the past behind me and move on, I was still intimidated by Doug. Having Miles by my side with Jackson and their other friend Asher standing behind us helped, but it was hard to break old patterns. "I'm sorry..."

"Hell right you are," Doug said.

"Shut the fuck up and let her talk or I'll take an incredible amount of pleasure from silencing you for good," Miles threatened.

"I'm sorry I didn't see you for the person you are years ago," I said. "If I had, it would have saved me so much time."

Doug swallowed, his Adam's apple bobbing up and down in his scrawny throat. "What are you doing, Kins? Come inside and let's talk this through."

I shook my head. "We're done. I don't want you to contact me again. Tell your friends and family what you want, but pull that missing person report. If you don't, I'll tell my side of the story, and I doubt you want that on the evening news."

The moment stretched. There were so many other things I could say to him, but he wasn't worth the effort it would take to spit out the words.

"Is there anything else?" Miles asked, his gaze still pinning Doug in place.

"I'd like to go in and grab a few of my things."

Miles stepped into the foyer and herded Doug

away from the door. "Why don't you go get what you need while I keep this asshole company right here?"

"None of this shit is yours. I paid for everything." Doug's voice followed me up the stairs. I hated the fact that he was right. I didn't own a damn thing except my name.

A quiet meow came from behind the door of the bedroom. I opened it and gathered the cat I'd rescued a couple of years ago up in my arms. I'd named her Hope, and she'd been my only confidante. I couldn't leave her here.

There was only one other thing I wanted. I sat down on the bed and pulled open the drawer of my nightstand, searching for the picture of my mom, dad, and me. It was my most treasured possession, and Doug knew it. With one hand wrapped around Hope, I rummaged through the drawer but came up empty. It was gone.

"Don't even think about taking that damn cat." Doug's voice had a panicked edge to it. The best thing to do would be to leave as quickly as possible before he lost control. If anything happened to Miles because of me, I'd never forgive myself.

"You don't even like cats. She's coming with me." I grabbed my purse from the coat closet and walked down the steps with Hope in my arms. At least I had my phone, ID, and a little bit of cash in my wallet.

Miles arched a brow. "Is that everything you wanted?"

I nodded.

"Kinley, why don't you go wait in the truck so Doug and I can come to a quick understanding about what's going to happen next?" He tilted his head toward the door. "Keys are in it. Go ahead and start it so you and the cat stay warm. This will only take a second."

"You walk out that door now, and I'll never take you back," Doug threatened.

Miles shook his head. "I'm the one who's going to be making the threats. You got it?"

I let the door close behind me but stayed on the stoop. Miles came out a few moments later, his eyes lighting up with surprise when he saw me standing there.

"What did you do to him?" I asked, more worried about Miles being hurt or getting in trouble than what might have happened to my asshole ex.

"Nothing more than he did to you." Miles took my elbow and gently led me toward the truck at the curb.

Doug burst through the door. He was unharmed except for the area around his left eye. "That's it, run away."

Miles let go of my elbow and nodded to Asher. "Can you help Kinley into the truck while Jackson and I have a final word with this jerk?"

"Forget it." Doug scrambled back toward the door and poked his head out of the doorway. "You'll be back, Kinley. If you want that picture of yours, I know you will."

"Are you sure you have everything?" Miles put a hand on my shoulder.

"We should go." No telling what Doug might do now that his fragile ego had been threatened. As much as I mourned the loss of my one piece of the past, it wasn't worth putting Miles, Asher, and Jackson at risk. I took a final look at the place where I'd tried to build a home and turned my back. I was on my own now.

"ARE YOU OKAY?" Kinley asked.

"I'm fine."

She'd been quiet the entire drive back to Mustang Mountain and hadn't said a word until I dropped Jackson and Asher off where they'd left their trucks. I owed both of them for going with me this afternoon, though none of the guys kept track. Being part of the Mustang Mountain Riders meant we always had each other's backs.

"How are you feeling after what went down?" I eased the truck away from the curb and headed into town. We hadn't talked about what would happen after we picked up her things, but since she'd left everything behind, she was going to need a few necessities.

"Relieved, but also terrified," she said. Then followed with a huge sigh. "I've never seen anyone stand up to Doug before. I think you caught him by surprise."

"Maybe if someone had taken him down a few pegs a long time ago, he might have learned the proper way to treat a woman." I glanced over, hoping my offhand remark hadn't made her mad. "Sorry. It just pisses me off, knowing he had his hands on you."

"You don't have to apologize. I shouldn't have stayed for so long. I've just never had anyone take my side before." She glanced down at the cat sleeping on her lap.

"You don't have to answer, but what kind of picture does he have of yours?" I worried he might have some photo he'd use to blackmail her.

"It's just a picture of me with my mom and dad. I lost my dad when I was just a kid and my mom passed from cancer a couple of years ago. I know it seems like a small thing, but he knows how important it is to me."

I barely knew her, but there was something about her that made me want to be the man she needed—the man she deserved. "I'm on your side now, Kinley, and I'll do whatever I can to help you get it back."

"Thank you, but you've already done so much." Her words came out barely over a whisper. "You probably ought to call that woman so I can meet up with someone at the shelter. I'm sure you've got other things you'd rather be doing than running me all over Montana and getting into fist fights."

I didn't want her to go to the shelter. If her ex decided he wanted her back, there wouldn't be anyone to protect her. I had no right to feel possessive of her, but I did.

"Do you want me to call?" I offered.

She bit her lip and ran her hand over the cat's back. Damn lucky cat. I couldn't help but be a little jealous. What would it be like to have her soft hands running over my skin? It wasn't right to think that way, especially after what she'd been through. I couldn't control the way I felt, but I could keep a tight lid on my attraction.

"It would probably be best," she finally said. "I'm not sure if they'd let me bring Hope, though."

I pulled up the number I'd called last night on my phone screen but couldn't bring myself to connect the call. "If you'd rather stay at my place until you figure things out, you wouldn't have to worry about whether they'd let you bring the cat."

"You mean it?" Her head snapped up to meet my gaze.

She was looking at me like some kind of hero. My chest tightened at the hopeful glimmer in her eyes. "I've got the space. As long as you don't mind putting up with me."

Her fingers curled around my forearm. Even through my thick coat, I could feel the pressure of her touch. "If you're sure it's no trouble, I'd really appreciate it. Thinking about trying to start over in a new place where I don't know anyone is stressing me out. And if I had to give up Hope right now..."

"It's settled. Let's run into the mercantile to get some cat food and whatever else she'll need."

"I can cook and clean to earn my keep, and I'll pay you back for whatever you spend on stuff for me and Hope." Kinley pulled her hand away to tuck the cat into her bag.

"You don't owe me anything. Just pay it forward and we'll call it good. How does that sound?"

"You're one of the good ones, Miles."

No one had ever referred to me like that. In that moment, I vowed I'd do whatever it would take to be worthy of her compliments. "You'd better cut that out before you make me blush."

"I bet you're pretty darn cute when you blush." A soft laugh spilled from her lips, catching us both off guard.

Shaking the feeling away, I pulled into a parking spot on the street, then walked around to her side of the truck and helped her down. Together, we stepped into the Nelson Mercantile. Ruby and Orville had been running the one-stop shop on Main for decades. I grabbed a basket and walked to the back corner where they kept pet supplies, hoping Orville would be behind the counter tonight, so I didn't have to face Ruby. When Jackson and Emma stopped by this morning, they broke the news that Ruby had picked me to be her mountain man for March. As soon as I made sure Kinley was settled, I planned on confronting Ruby about it, but tonight wasn't the night.

"What kind of food do you think she likes?" I asked.

"This one." Kinley gathered a few cans of wet cat food. "I'll get some dry too."

"Miles! I was hoping you'd stop by soon." Ruby stood at the end of the aisle looking like a cat herself... the kind of cat who was about to chow down on the canary. "Who do we have here?"

I could practically see the wheels turning in her head. Unless I wanted to be the focus of her next town update, I needed to nip whatever ideas she was putting together right in the bud.

"Hey, Ruby. This is Kinley. She's new in town, and I'm helping her get settled."

"Kinley,"—Ruby reached out and put a hand on Kinley's shoulder—"I heard your fiance broke off the wedding. I'm so sorry, dear. I didn't realize you were planning on sticking around. Where are you staying?"

I was on the verge of telling Ruby to mind her own damn business, but Kinley was way ahead of me. Her lips curled up into a dazzling smile.

"It's nice to meet you. I've been told you're the one who can tell me what's really going on around town."

Ruby stood up straighter. "I like to stay informed. As the mayor's wife, I'm obligated to keep track of all the major news."

"I don't suppose you know of anyone who might be hiring?" Kinley asked.

"Why don't you let me treat you to a cup of coffee and we can chat about what you might be looking for?" Ruby steered Kinley toward the counter at the front.

"Miles can finish the shopping while we talk. Isn't that right, Miles?"

"It would be my pleasure." I sure hoped Kinley knew what she was getting herself into by talking to Ruby. While they gabbed over an entire pot of coffee, I gathered a few things I'd been meaning to pick up on my next trip into town, along with some items I thought Kinley might need. I'd never lived with a woman before except for my sister, and I hadn't paid too much attention to her.

"Guess what?" Kinley found me in the toothbrush aisle where I was trying to decide if she'd prefer a medium or soft bristle.

"What?" I tossed the soft bristled brush into the basket and turned to face her.

"I think I got a job." She bounced up and down on her toes, clearly excited about the lead.

"Where?" No telling what Ruby might have suggested.

"The hair place down the street. Ruby said the owner, Noelle, is looking for someone to answer the phones and help out around the salon. I always thought it would be fun to go to cosmetology school. Ruby even has an old truck I can borrow until I can afford a car."

"That's great." I knew exactly what truck Ruby offered. It had been sitting in their drive for the past two years. I'd have to get one of the guys to look at it before Kinley could drive it. Best case would mean new tires if she wanted to be able to get up and down the mountain without sliding off the road. Worst case would mean a whole new engine. She looked so happy at the thought of getting a job. I wouldn't say anything to bring her down tonight.

Ruby came around the corner with a small piece of paper in her hand. "Here's Noelle's number. Give her a call in the morning and the two of you can figure out a time to meet up."

"Thank you so much." Kinley reached out and pulled Ruby into a hug.

"You're more than welcome. Any new friend of Miles's is a friend to all of us." Ruby narrowed her eyes at me over Kinley's shoulder. "I hope it works out and that you'll be sticking around for a while."

"Oh, I hope so too." Kinley gave her a final squeeze before releasing her.

"Should we take this stuff to the front so you can ring it up?" I was eager to get out of there before Ruby started asking more questions.

"Orville's at the register. I hope you'll stop by after you meet with Noelle to let me know how it goes."

"I will." Kinley couldn't seem to stop smiling. My cheeks hurt just from looking at her, though it warmed my heart to see her so happy.

"I'm already looking forward to it."

I'd need to warn Kinley about Ruby and her meddling ways before they sat down together again. Ruby might be the mayor's wife and a good person to turn to in a time of crisis, but she was also single-handedly responsible for running the Mustang Mountain rumor mill. No doubt half the town would be well aware that I had a woman moving in with me before we even made our way out the door.

MILES RAN me into town a couple of days later and dropped me off at the Best Little Hair House. I was self-conscious of the black and blue bruise covering my cheek, but Noelle was just as nice as everyone else I'd met in Mustang Mountain. We only chatted for about fifteen minutes before she offered me the job. I couldn't wait to start in a few days. It might not be my dream job, but it was definitely a step in the right direction. Miles said he had some errands to run while I talked to Noelle, so I stopped by the mercantile to wait for him.

"I hear congratulations are in order." Ruby rested her arms on the counter and leaned toward me. "Can I get you a cup of coffee to celebrate?"

"Oh, that's okay. I'm just waiting for Miles." He'd warned me that in a town the size of Mustang Mountain, word traveled fast. I didn't expect the news of my new job to beat me down the street, though.

Ruby moved to the coffeepot and filled a mug. "Here, it's on the house."

"Thank you." I added sugar and cream, then took a sip.

"So tell me... what's going on between you and Miles?" Her tone sounded innocent enough, but the curiosity in her eyes was more than casual. "He doesn't know it yet, but he's the Mountain Man of the Month."

"Oh? What does that mean?"

She pulled a flyer out from under the counter and set it in front of me. A picture of a shirtless Miles was plastered across the front. I knew he was strong, but seeing the ridges of his abs and the bulge of his muscles in full color sent heat racing to the apex of my thighs.

"I'm on a personal mission to get the single men around here hitched." She crossed her arms under her ample bosom. "You're either going to take him off the market if the two of you get involved, or prevent him from getting close to someone if you're just using him for room and board. Which is it?"

I wasn't used to people prying into my personal life. "Um, I just walked away from my own wedding. I'm not looking for a relationship so soon."

Ruby's head bobbed up and down. "That's what I figured. We ought to get you out of there so he can focus on the women who've expressed interest. I'll make a few calls and see if I can get you set up somewhere else. Now that you've got the truck, you'll have a way to get around, too."

"Thank you." The mug rattled on its saucer as I

hooked my finger through the handle. Miles made it sound like I wouldn't be in the way, but maybe he just didn't want me to feel bad.

"Here he is now." Ruby slid the flyer off the counter. "Best not to tell him he's been selected. I want to break the news in a big way."

"Of course."

"Hey, how did it go?" Miles stopped behind me. "Can I get a cup of that coffee too, Ruby?"

I'd been looking forward to sharing my good news, but the conversation with Ruby had drained a little of my enthusiasm. "Good. I got the job."

"Congratulations. When do you start?" His lips spread into a wide grin, and he lifted his mug to clink against mine. So that's what it felt like to have someone share in my success. I wasn't under the impression that securing a job answering phones was a great accomplishment, but it would be the first job I'd had since high school. Miles seemed to be able to appreciate that fact.

"Thursday. She said I could come in for a few hours Thursday and Friday, so I'd be ready to pull a full shift on Saturday."

"I should take you out to dinner to celebrate." His giant hand settled on my shoulder. Warmth traveled all the way down to my toes at the contact. I couldn't help but picture the image of his naked chest that had been seared on my brain. "Want me to call the guys to see if they want to join us?"

"I should be the one taking you out to dinner." I'd

never be able to repay him for his kindness, but I could do the next best thing and get out of his cabin so he could continue his search for someone who could give him the kind of attention he deserved.

His phone rang, interrupting the conversation. "Sorry, I should get this."

"Go ahead." I turned to face forward again, keeping my focus on the mug in front of me like it held the answers to all of my problems.

"That was Asher. He needs a hand with a horse he's trying to rescue." He pulled his keys out of his pocket. "Do you want to take my truck home, and I'll have him bring me back when we're done?"

The word *home* rang through my head. He'd tossed it out there so casually, like it didn't mean a thing. I couldn't let myself start thinking about his place as home. It was too tempting. "You want me to drive up the mountain?"

"Well, the truck won't drive itself, Kinley." He chuckled.

"Sure." I took the keys and marveled at his ability to trust a stranger.

"I'll see you in a little while. Congratulations again on getting that job. I knew you could do it." He gave my shoulder a squeeze, then tossed a couple of bills down on the counter before heading toward the front of the store.

I sat in silence for a bit while I finished my coffee. There was no way I'd let him take me out to dinner to celebrate, but I could make him dinner at his place.

Then we could figure out the best way for me to get out of his life before I got too used to him.

Miles

ASHER HAD JUST DROPPED me off after I'd spent the afternoon helping him get an injured horse over to his place. It was the first time I'd returned to find to smoke drifting from my chimney and the warm glow of lights on in my kitchen. My place didn't just look like a cabin in the woods; it looked like a home.

I pushed open the front door and the smell of something amazing made my mouth water. "What smells so good?"

"I'm making dinner." Kinley called out from the kitchen. Soft country music played in the background.

I stopped in the family room, where Hope curled up on the thick rug in front of the fire. She cracked an eyelid open as I squatted down to run my hand over her back. We'd had a cat when I was younger, though since I'd moved out on my own I'd never been tempted to make a long-term commitment to an animal. I'd gotten used to coming home to an empty house, but I kind of liked the idea of coming home to a fire in the fireplace and something bubbling on the stove.

"Can I get you a glass of wine?" Kinley asked. There was something different about her voice. She sounded lighter, even happy. "Do you even drink wine? I guess I should have asked before I opened up a bottle, but I needed a splash for the roast."

I left the cat stretching out on the rug and wandered toward the kitchen, not sure what I would find. I'd never had someone cook dinner for me at my own house before.

"What's going on here?" I paused in the doorway. She had two pots on the stove and something in the oven. My mouth watered as the unmistakable scent of homemade pot roast filled my nose.

"I'm making you dinner to thank you for letting me stay." She looked over from where she stood at the stove, one hand shoved into a giant oven mitt, the other gripping a large serving fork. "I couldn't find a potato ricer in your utensil drawer."

"What's a potato ricer?" I moved closer to get a better look.

"To mash the potatoes. Don't you ever cook?" She smiled, the kind of grin that lit me up inside.

"Not unless it's absolutely necessary." I snagged a piece of meat from the platter next to her. "You didn't have to do this, but I'm glad you did."

"Well, you didn't have to bring me home with you, but I'm glad you did that, too." She pulled her hand out of the oven mitt and brushed the hair away from her face. "Next time we go into town, I'm buying you a proper masher."

"Let me help." I nudged my hip into hers and gently bumped her out of the way.

"Go for it. I'm working up a sweat." Her cheeks flushed, and she fanned herself with the oven mitt before handing it over. "It's probably the wine."

"What kind of wine did you buy?" I kept my eyes trained on Kinley as I smashed the soft potatoes at the bottom of the pot. Her hair hung over her shoulders in two long braids and she had on one of my old t-shirts and a pair of jeans Emma had given her. Both hung loose but didn't begin to hide the curve of her hips or the swell of her breasts.

She shrugged. "I don't know. Some kind of red blend. Want a taste?"

"Sure."

"Here, try mine." She held out her wine glass. "Wait. Don't stop mashing. I'll tip it up so you can take a sip."

She stepped close and lifted the glass. My skin prickled with awareness. This close I could see the flecks of gold in her big brown eyes. She touched the rim of the glass to my lips, and our eyes met. I forgot about mashing potatoes and let the serving fork fall from my hand.

Wine spilled into my mouth as I wrapped my arm around her back to pull her against me. I was probably ruining everything, but I wasn't thinking. My body was reacting to having her inside my personal space. I had a tendency to hold people at a distance, but I didn't want to keep Kinley away. I wanted her close. Wanted to nudge my nose into her hair and breathe in her scent. Wanted to do a hell of a lot more with her, too. Like show her what it would be like to be with a man who could appreciate her and wouldn't take her for granted.

She pulled the wine glass away and stared up at me, her eyes round. Leave it to me to scare her. I let my eyelids close while I drew in a deep breath and loosened my grip. When I opened my eyes, she stared up at me, but there was no fear looking back.. All I saw was the same feeling I'd felt deep in my gut... the same feeling I'd been fighting since I met her... need.

"You've got a little wine on your—"

"Where?" I lifted a finger to wipe it away, but she shook her head.

"I'll get it." The tip of her tongue swept out to lick the drop of wine at the corner of my mouth away. The second I felt her touch, my grip tightened around her.

I wasn't sure who kissed who first, but our mouths collided. My tongue slipped past her lips and my first taste of her sent blood racing straight to my cock. I was immediately desperate for more.

She must have felt the same. Her hands slid over my shoulders and she clasped her fingers together behind my neck. I became acutely aware of every place our bodies touched... her breasts smashing against my chest, her hips pressed against my thighs, her fingers digging into my skin. This was the kind of moment I could lose myself in forever. Though now that I was finally touching her, forever didn't seem nearly long enough.

Somehow, I summoned enough self-control to back away. She didn't need me coming onto her while she was so vulnerable. "I'm sorry, Kinley. I shouldn't have done that."

Her chest heaved with short breaths as we broke apart. "Don't be."

"It's been a long time for me, and it's not fair for me to take advantage."

"Is that what you think is happening here?" She squinted up at me, her lips curling into a grin.

I'd never pretend to understand the inner workings of a woman's mind, but her reaction wasn't what I was expecting. "Well, yeah. I let my attraction get the best of me. It won't happen again."

"That's too bad."

"Excuse me?"

"I've spent the last five years feeling like an inconvenience, being treated like an afterthought. We might not have known each other long, but you've never made me feel like less, Miles. When you look at me, I feel like you actually see me."

I saw her alright. Saw the gorgeous woman she was on the outside as well as within. Saw the way she treated people with care and consideration. Saw the way she'd turned my cabin into a home instead of just a place where I lived and worked and slept.

"I see you, baby." Cupping her cheek with one hand, I backed her up against the kitchen counter. "I see you and I've never wanted anyone more."

"Show me, then. Show me what it feels like to be wanted."

HIS IRISES DARKENED, and he pushed his hips into me. I could feel his need nudging against my belly. I was playing with fire, but I couldn't care less if I got burned. It had been too long since I'd been attracted to anyone. Now, the desire coursing through my veins felt like it would consume me.

Hungry lips descended on mine. I barely caught my breath before he slid his tongue into my mouth. The dinner I'd spent so long preparing faded into the background. All that mattered was finding a way to quell the desperate ache throbbing between my legs.

His hands slipped under my shirt while my fingers fumbled with the button of his jeans. My pulse spiked as his fingers skimmed over my sides.

"We don't have to do anything you don't want to." His voice sounded raw, like he was caught off guard as much as I was by what was happening between us.

"I want this. I want you." It had been so long since

anyone made me feel anything. Maybe I was foolish to jump from Doug's arms into Miles's, but I hadn't been emotionally invested in my ex in years. What I felt for Miles was as real as it got. In that moment, I felt desirable, and I'd do anything to hold on to that feeling as long as I could.

He undid my bra and slid his hands around my ribcage. Every brush of his skin against mine sent another wave of goosebumps down my arms. My nipples tightened into two hard buds as his t-shirt glided over them. Then his mouth left mine. I opened my eyes to see him lean over right before he sucked one of my nipples into his mouth.

A moan ripped loose from the back of my throat. I didn't know I was capable of the feelings he brought on. He seemed to know how to play my body like an instrument only he had mastered.

"Damn, baby, you taste so good." His mouth switched to my other breast. Heat shot down my spine and my hips ground against his cock. I'd never been so forward, never felt the desperate hollowness between my legs like I did with him.

"Come here." Miles backed me toward the kitchen table. He'd told me it was made out of a fir tree he'd cut down himself on the side of the mountain. I just hoped it was as sturdy as it looked, especially when he lifted my ass up onto the edge and finished pulling my pants down my legs.

"Condom?" I mumbled.

"Already working on it." He rummaged through a

drawer and came up with an unopened box. Then he kicked off his pants.

I propped myself up on my elbows to get a glimpse of what I could expect. My breath froze mid-inhale as his cock sprang free. My brief moment of panic was replaced with anticipation. He stroked himself a couple of times before he unrolled the condom down his length.

"Last chance to turn back."

The warning didn't dissuade me, it spurred me on. There was no way I was backing out now. Not after seeing the preview.

I shook my head and leaned back on the cold slab of wood. "I'm done looking back. It's time for me to move forward."

He pulled me to the edge. With my ass hanging halfway off the table, he leaned over and rested a palm flat on the wood on either side of my head. "I'm really glad you feel that way, Kinley."

Soft kisses landed on my stomach as he made his way up to my lips. I was already ready—my panties had been damp since seeing that picture earlier—but the way he circled my clit with his thick finger had me hovering at the edge. When I didn't think I could take another second of his teasing, the tip of his cock nudged at my entrance. Pleasure surged through me. I clasped my ankles together behind his ass and urged him to take me.

"Come with me, baby." His hips pumped as his cock stroked my g-spot over and over.

I wanted to tell him I was already there, but my brain had lost its connection with my mouth. When I tried to speak, the only thing that came out of me was a low, strangled moan. I dug my fingers into his shoulders and held on for dear life as I came apart around him.

"COME HERE, BABY." Miles held out a hand to help me up. "I'm sorry we didn't get to eat dinner while it was hot."

"You don't look very sorry," I teased. A smug, satisfied grin spread across those lips that had explored every inch of my skin. I wasn't a small girl, so he'd covered a lot of real estate.

"You're right. I'm not." His arms wrapped around me, pulling me up against his chest. "You need to put something on so you're not cold."

"I'm pretty sure you'll keep me warm enough."

His lips sought mine, and he gave me a long, lingering kiss. "Are you hungry?"

"Starving." I tilted my head back to stare into his eyes. He might be too good to be true, but I wasn't ready to admit it. I didn't want to give him up, not now that I'd finally found someone who didn't look at me like I was a complete and utter failure.

"I know it won't be nearly as good, but how about I heat up dinner in the microwave for us?"

"That's the good thing about a pot roast. It tastes even better the second time around."

"Oh yeah?" Miles kept his hands clasped behind my back as he walked toward the counter. "I have the feeling the same's true about you."

My laugh bubbled up through my chest. I loved this playful part of his personality. Not only was he kind, caring, and built like the Rock's blond, much younger brother, he also had a sense of humor. "When did you turn into such a flirt?"

"You must bring out that side of me."

I turned around so his chest pressed against my back. "How many sides do you have?"

His hands slid up my belly until he cupped one of my breasts in each palm. My nipples tightened. I could feel his cock growing hard again.

"How hungry are you, baby?"

I could already tell where this was headed, and I was all for it. "Not so hungry that I can't be distracted for a little bit."

He kissed along the column of my neck, his cock pressing into my core. "I'm going to take you slow this time, baby... the way I should have before."

My nerve endings fired up and down my side, tiny sparks of pleasure like little signs of what was to come. He could take me however he wanted. I'd never felt so cherished, and I didn't want the feeling to end.

"Let's go to bed." He pulled away like it physically pained him to break the connection. "I want to spread you out so I can take my time."

A thrill raced through me at the grit in his tone. I held tight to his hand as he led me to the bedroom and lifted me onto the bed. He fluffed a pillow and handed it to me.

"Make yourself comfortable. We're going to be here a while." Then he climbed on the bed and hovered over me. His lips trailed kisses from my forehead to my chin, then down to my collarbone. "Do you have any idea how beautiful you are? How much I want you?"

I couldn't keep my hands off him, couldn't stop from running my fingers over his arms. As he moved down my body, his biceps flexed. He was a physical masterpiece, and he wanted me... the girl with the wide hips and big ass who'd spent most of her life trying to hide her curves.

His kisses continued between my breasts and over my belly. The whole time he mumbled compliments against my skin. How hard I made him... how soft my skin was... how he couldn't wait to taste me... how he'd been fantasizing about me riding his cock since the moment we met. He moved even lower, using his shoulders to spread my thighs until I sprawled out underneath him, totally bare.

It was too much. Between his words, his warm breath on my thighs, and his tongue delving deep into my core, I couldn't take any more. "I don't think I can, Miles. It's too intense."

"Hold on, baby, I've got you." He shifted his attention to suck on my clit.

Stars exploded behind my eyelids as he coaxed me to my second release. He was in total control, and he knew it. I couldn't move, couldn't think, couldn't make any sense of the sensations rocketing through me.

When I finally came down, he crawled up my body and captured my mouth in a kiss. "You look like an angel when you come."

I kissed him back with everything I had. Then I rolled over on top of him, determined to make him feel at least half as incredible. As I closed my lips around the tip of his cock, his eyes widened. Then I took him deep into my mouth until he hit the back of my throat and I almost gagged.

His hands went to my hair, and I could tell he was holding back. I slid up and down, using my lips and my tongue to drive him to the edge.

"Kinley, I'm close, baby."

"I know. I've got you." Knowing he'd said the same words to me right before I gave into my release cemented what was happening between us. I could be vulnerable with him, just like he could trust enough to let down his guard with me. I'd found my person. With Miles in my heart, I'd never be alone again.

I COULDN'T REMEMBER a time in my life when I'd ever felt so fucking happy. Even my clients noticed it. I'd just hung up on a video call with the president of a company who'd hired me to create a custom software solution and even he commented on my new attitude. I told him it was all the fresh mountain air that had me in a good mood, but it had nothing to do with the elements and everything to do with a certain curvy angel who'd been sharing my bed.

She'd been living with me for two weeks. Long enough for me to know that I never wanted to be without her. I'd even hacked into the visitor bureau website and pulled the fucking bachelor profile Ruby set up for me. Kinley was it for me.

I ran my hand over Hope's back. The cat had taken to sitting in my lap while I worked on my computer all day. I've never thought of myself as a cat guy, but she'd charmed her way into my heart. She'd even made friends with Hades. I got up and set her on the ground. She looked up at me, a little miffed at having her nap interrupted.

"Sorry, girl. If I leave now, I can make it to town in time to take your mama some lunch."

Hope just flicked her tail in the air and strutted out to the family room. Evidently, I was a man who talked to cats now. Kinley had changed me in more ways than I could have imagined. I was also a man who'd rearrange his entire schedule to spend a few minutes with the woman he loved.

Damn. There it was. The "L" word popped into my head with no warning. I waited for my chest to tighten or for my vision to start going black around the edges. Instead, a peaceful knowing settled in my heart. I loved her. Now that I realized it, I couldn't wait to tell her.

"I'll be back, Hope. Don't get into any trouble while I'm gone." I glanced over to where she sat in front of the door leading out to the deck. Hades stood on the other side of the glass. He'd taken to visiting every day around this time so they could stare at each other through the window. The first time I saw him there, I thought he might think of her as a meal, but the more he showed up, the more I realized he just wanted to play.

Funny how things worked out sometimes. If a wolf and a cat could become friends, maybe I had it in me to open my heart up to someone.

.   .   .

A HALF HOUR LATER, I stood in line at the diner to pick up the order I'd called in on my way down the mountain. Kinley had become pretty fond of their bison burger with huckleberry sauce, and I wanted to surprise her by bringing her lunch at the salon.

"Hey, what are you doing here?" Emma hip checked me as she stepped into line. "Is my big brother playing hooky from work?"

I turned and gave her a sloppy half hug. "Just stopping in to take lunch over to Kinley."

"The two of you are getting pretty serious, aren't you?" She'd always been able to read me. It wasn't worth trying to hide the truth, especially since I planned on letting everyone know Kinley and I were together as soon as I told her I loved her and made sure she felt the same.

"So what if we are? I thought you liked her?" The two of them had become fast friends, especially since Emma and Jackson were the only ones living on the same road, and we'd been getting together pretty often.

"Oh, I do. She's fantastic." Emma squeezed my arm.

"But?"

She bit her lip. "No buts."

"Come on, Em. I can tell you're holding back."

"It's just... I don't know how to say it..."

"Spit it out. You know I can take it." Better to hear her out and head off any concerns now.

Emma tilted her head and screwed her lips into a

frown. "Do you ever worry that you're just filling her ex's shoes?"

"What the hell? You think I'm the same as that deadbeat who got off on taking advantage of her? That's low, sis." My gut pitched and rolled. I'd expected better from my sister. We might not have always been close, but she knew who I was at my core.

"No, that's not what I'm saying at all." Emma wrapped her fingers around my arm. "She's young, Miles. I'm just a little worried that she's never been on her own. She moved straight from his place into yours. I mean, you know her better than anyone, so I could be way off base."

I wanted to blow her off, but she'd hit on something that had been pinging at the back of my mind. Kinley had changed so much since I'd met her. She'd jumped into the cab of my truck with tears streaming down her cheeks, afraid of her own shadow. Over the past couple of weeks, she'd grown more confident, put herself out there and got a job, and had even talked to her boss about starting cosmetology school.

I knew she cared about me. The kind of chemistry we had together couldn't be faked. But what if Emma was right? What if she'd traded her ex for me because I was safe?

"What are you saying? You think she needs to be on her own?"

"I don't know, but I think you might want to bring it up. She obviously cares about you. I can see it in the way she looks at you when she thinks no one else is watching. I just want to make sure she's with you for the right reasons." Emma nudged her elbow into my ribs. "Just think about it. I want you to find the kind of happiness I've found with Jackson, and I don't want either one of you to get hurt."

The lightness I'd been feeling earlier faded away and a heavy weight settled in my chest. I grabbed the bag of takeout from the counter and turned toward Emma. She had that look in her eyes like she regretted giving voice to her concerns.

"I'm sorry." She shifted her weight from one foot to the other. "That was probably way out of line."

"Nah. I told you, I can take it. Thanks for your concern. I know you've got my best interests at heart." I put my hand on top of her head and ruffled her blonde waves. "Give Jackson a fist bump from me, okay?"

"Miles..."

"I'm fine. I've got a burger to deliver before it gets cold." Even though it wouldn't take more than a minute to make the walk down the street to the salon, I needed to get the hell out of there. Needed to get my head on straight before I saw Kinley. "See ya around."

I left Emma standing in line and pushed through the door out into the crisp mountain air. Emma brought up some valid concerns, but it didn't mean Kinley and I weren't supposed to be together. I'd planned on springing those three little words on her today. It might make more sense to have a conversation and shut down Emma's worries for good.

"YOU'RE THE BEST, the absolute best of the best." I stood on my tiptoes and pressed a kiss to Miles's scruffy cheek as my fingers closed around the handles of the plastic bag. "Do you have time to stick around for lunch? I've got twenty minutes."

"Did your lunchtime hero bring burgers for all of us?" Noelle walked by, her perfect brows arched.

"Find your own mountain man. This one's mine." I linked my arm with Miles's and beamed up at him. "She's taking inventory in the back room, but we could sit in the truck."

"Yeah, let's do it." He grinned back, but something was off.

He walked ahead to open the passenger side door and held the bag of food while I climbed up inside.

"Thanks for bringing me lunch." I could tell he'd brought my favorite by the intoxicating scent of charbroiled beef and the sweet smell of huckleberry sauce. "You take such good care of me."

"Someone's got to," he teased.

"Very funny." I set the bag of fries on the console while he walked around the truck to slide behind the wheel. "Did you eat?"

"Not yet. I'll grab something when I get home."

"How can you say no to this burger?" Mustang Mountain might be small, but they had some of the best food I'd ever had in my life.

Miles didn't answer, just sat there drumming his fingers on the steering wheel. Something was bothering him. I licked a drop of huckleberry compote from the corner of my mouth as I grabbed a fry.

"Did something happen with work today?" I didn't fully understand what he did on a daily basis, though I knew he created computer programs for companies. Big companies with big budgets based on what I'd gathered.

"It's... hell, Kinley... I've just been thinking about us. Thinking about what you've been through and what's best for your future." A muscle in his jaw twitched.

I didn't like where this conversation was headed. Didn't like it at all. I set the burger down and angled my upper body to face him. "My future?"

"Yeah. You don't want to spend the rest of your life driving up and down the mountain to sweep up hair, do you?" He glanced over at me, and I didn't recognize the look in his eyes.

"I haven't really thought much about it. Yes, I've looked into cosmetology school, but the closest one is in Missoula. Noelle thinks it would be a good move, but..."

His brows pulled together. "But what?"

"But it's too far of a drive to make every day. The program runs for months." I didn't like feeling like I needed to defend myself. It reminded me too much of everything I'd been through with my ex. He'd constantly questioned me and made me feel like I wasn't good enough for him. I thought Miles was above that.

"Is that what you want to do?"

He was talking in circles. "What do you mean? Are you asking if I want to move to Missoula and start cosmetology school?"

"Yeah."

I wasn't going to lie and say the thought hadn't crossed my mind, but I was happy. Happier than I'd been in a long, long time. But what if that was what he wanted? Black dots danced across my vision. I blinked, trying to focus on Miles. "Do you want me to go?"

"No." He slowly shook his head back and forth. At least he was quick to answer. But the hesitation in his eyes wasn't what I expected from a man I'd already fallen for. "I want you to do what's best for you. I don't want to be your safety net. I don't want you to trade one relationship for another because it's the safe thing to do."

"You think I'm playing it safe by being with you?"

The past couple of weeks had been heaven on earth. I couldn't understand why he was questioning things. Unless… unless I'd been misreading the entire situation the whole time we'd been together. I dug my fingernails into my palm while I waited for him to answer.

"I don't know."

"If you're tired of me mooching off of you, just say so." We'd talked about money briefly. I had every intention of pitching in on expenses as soon as I could, but he'd assured me he made more money than he'd ever be able to spend in this lifetime, and it wasn't a concern.

"That's not it at all."

My patience was wearing thin. "Then what are you trying to say?"

He reached up and pinched the bridge of his nose. "I'm saying maybe you need some time on your own to figure out what you really want. I care about you a lot, Kinley, but I don't want to be your rebound guy."

Unbelievable. He'd been building me up for the past few weeks, and now he'd pulled the rug right out from under me. "My rebound guy? Are you serious? You've done more for me in the short time I've known you than anyone's ever done for me before. You know what I think?"

"What's that?" He turned those blue eyes on me and I almost lost my nerve.

"I think you're starting to realize I might not be good enough for you. Maybe it was fun to feel like a knight in shining armor who swooped in to save a damsel in distress, but now that the big, bad dragon has been slayed, you realize you got the scullery maid instead of the princess." I couldn't breathe. The air in the cab of the truck was too thick and heavy to take in.

"Don't be ridiculous, Kinley."

The dismissive tone in his voice was the last straw. When I walked out on Doug, I'd promised myself I wouldn't let a man make me feel like less again. Yet there I was. I had to get out of the truck. My fingers fumbled with the door handle, suddenly too stiff and awkward to set myself free.

"Where are you going?"

I stood on the pavement next to the truck. "I can't be with someone who doesn't want to be with me."

Miles leaned across the console. "I never said I didn't want to be with you. Let's be serious about this."

"Oh, I am being serious. Maybe for the first time in my life. I'm sorry to have put you out for so long. I hope you find what you're looking for someday, Miles." I slammed the door and stomped back into the salon. Tears poured from my eyes and snot filled my nose. I hated feeling this way.

"You okay, hon?" Noelle glanced up from where she was writing something down in the appointment book.

"Yeah." I stopped at the front counter. I was done depending on others. I'd wanted to stick around Mustang Mountain because of Miles, but he'd made it clear I needed to make something out of myself in order to be worthy of his time and attention. I was done trying to change myself for a man. It was time to do something for me. "You know that scholarship you mentioned for that school in Missoula?"

Noelle's eyes narrowed. "I thought you said you weren't interested, since it was so far away."

"Plans change." My lower lip trembled as I wiped away my tears. I'd wasted too many tears on men.

I hadn't known her long, but Noelle had become a good friend. "I'll text you the information. Are you sure about this?"

"Yeah. I think it's time I made some plans for my future." Plans that didn't revolve around a man. I thought Miles and I had something special, but it turned out I was a really bad judge of character. "By the way, do you happen to know of anywhere I could stay for a few days until I figure out what to do?"

"You're leaving Miles?"

"Looks that way."

"Oh, hon. I'm so sorry." Noelle slung her arm over my shoulders. "You're more than welcome to stay with me for a couple of days until you decide what to do."

"Thanks."

"Do you want to take the rest of the afternoon off?"

"I'd prefer to work." At least that might give me a fighting chance of keeping my mind from replaying every moment I'd spent with Miles.

Noelle rested her hand on my shoulder. "You got it, Kinley. I'll send that info over right now and the guest room is yours for as long as you need it."

I didn't trust myself to speak. My feelings were too fresh, my emotions too raw. I was done putting my hope and faith in others. I'd never let myself be vulnerable or risk having my heart broken again.

IN THE SPACE of a few weeks, I'd ruined everything. The mountains used to be my refuge, but that was before I knew what I'd been missing. I'd been trying to distract myself, but not even an early morning hike provided any respite. I used to love watching the sunrise over the peaks, but now all I wanted was to turn back time.

"Do you want to talk about it?" Asher asked. He sat a respectful dozen or so feet behind me, like he knew I needed that much space to breathe.

"No." I pulled the insulated tumbler of coffee from my daypack and took a sip. That just reminded me of sipping coffee with Kinley. How she measured by color, not ounces when she added cream to her mug. Everything reminded me of her. There was no escaping the memories. They were driving me out of my fucking mind.

"How's that been working out for you?" Asher's

boots crunched on the snow. Then he lowered himself down to sit next to me. "You haven't been at the club meetings and Jackson told me even your sister's starting to worry about you."

"I'm fine," I snapped. It had been a couple of weeks since Kinley left. A couple weeks of dragging myself out of bed and doing the bare minimum to make it through each day.

"You're not fine." Asher called things like he saw them. "And from what I hear, neither is she."

My gut twisted. "What do you mean? Have you talked to her?"

"No. But Emma has. She was telling us about it last night. If you'd come to the club meetings, you could have heard it yourself."

"What did she say?" I'd tried connecting with Kinley after that stupid fight we had. She ignored me. Except for the note she left me on the kitchen table when she came by to collect her things, I hadn't heard a word from her, and I didn't expect to. I'd blown it big time, and she was better off without me.

"Why not ask her yourself?"

"Because you're the one who mentioned it," I said. And because I didn't want to face my sister. Not when I still held a grudge about her questioning my relationship with Kinley in the first place. Obviously, if Kinley and I couldn't handle a conversation about our relationship, the bonds that held us together were much more fragile than I thought. But I hated when Emma was right. Especially when her being right coincided with me having my heart cut out of my chest and sent through a paper shredder. Though that visual was pretty damn accurate, it sent a chill through me.

"You're so fucking stubborn." Asher chuckled and took a sip of his own coffee.

"That's rich coming from you." All of my MC brothers had issues, but I was worried about Asher. We all had something we were hiding or something we were trying to escape by embracing the mountain life. Asher's reasons were still a mystery to me.

He angled his upper body my way.. "Sounds like she's doing great at that school in Missoula."

"Good." I didn't have to fake being happy for her. Knowing she was doing well made me feel like my heartache wasn't for nothing.

"It also sounds like she misses you." He turned to look at me.

I could feel the weight of his stare while I thought about how to respond. "Did she come right out and say that?"

"I'm just telling you what Emma said. If you're so interested, why the hell don't you try talking to Kinley about it?"

My jaw clenched. I didn't want to admit that if I heard her voice, I was afraid my shaky grip on holding myself together would shatter. "She made her choice."

"Based on what you told me, it sounds like she left because you made her feel like she wasn't good enough. You also accused her of not knowing her own heart and forced her to make an impossible choice."

Asher got to his feet and brushed the snow off his ass. "I'm heading back. I've got to check on a couple of the horses."

I didn't follow him. Not immediately. He might think his words were lost on a stubborn ass like me, but they'd hit close enough to home to have me questioning the way I'd handled things. Helping Kinley out of an awful situation felt good. I loved being the one she relied on. I'd never felt like a hero until she turned those big brown eyes on me and I coaxed a smile from her soft pink lips.

But Emma's words had messed with my head. She was just trying to protect me, the same way I would have tried to protect her. When it came down to it, I didn't want to be with a woman who needed to be with me. I wanted to be with a woman who had all the options in the world but still chose me. Not because I saved her, but because we were stronger together than we were apart.

Kinley never needed me to save her. All she needed was someone to point out the amazing woman she already was, someone who could help her see she was already capable of saving herself.

I'd been such a fool. I never considered how much stronger I felt with her by my side. She made me a better person just by being with me. For someone supposedly so smart, I felt like a complete and utter idiot.

Just as I was about to get to my feet and follow Asher down the trail I could take to get back to my cabin, there was a rustling in the trees a few hundred yards away.

Hades stepped out of the shadows, his muzzle crusted with snow. His head hung lower than usual as he headed my way. I hadn't seen him for several days. Right after Kinley left, he stopped by every day at the same time looking for Hope. When she didn't appear at the door for a few days in a row, he stopped coming.

"You miss them too, don't you?" I pulled off my glove so he could sniff my hand. He might act like a dog sometimes, but he was still a wild animal. His nose brushed the back of my hand, then he sat down next to me.

I ran my hand over the thick fur behind his ears.

"Do you think I'm an idiot for letting her go the way I did?" Everyone else seemed to have an opinion.

Hades nudged his head under my hand like he wanted me to keep scratching. We sat and watched the sun until the sky turned from light gray to purple to red and finally to a bright shade of warm yellow-orange.

Then I stood, finally ready to do what needed to be done. "I think it's time to go get them back."

Hades hopped to his feet and trotted next to me all the way back to the cabin.

I'D BEEN in Missoula for two weeks. Though I'd been enjoying the classes I'd been taking and was proud of myself for being on my own, I'd stopped trying to pretend I was happy. Being in the city was nice enough, and I'd been lucky to get into an apartment with two other girls who were in the same program. We got along well, but I missed Mustang Mountain. Even though I hadn't been there long, I missed working with Noelle. I missed having coffee with Emma and meeting up for dinner with Ford and Luna, too.

But most of all, I missed Miles.

Not a day went by that I didn't think about him or replay our last conversation in my head. There were so many things I wish I'd said. So many ways I could have handled myself without walking away and ending it for good. Looking back, I should have done more to reassure him it was him I wanted, not just some man to take care of me. I'd already come to that conclusion on my own, but hadn't communicated it very well to him.

It didn't matter now. He'd tried to reach out right after our fight, but classes were about to start, so I'd already left for Missoula. The scholarship I'd received covered my tuition and supplies, but I was responsible for my part of the rent and making the car payment on the new-to-me SUV I'd bought with some of the money I'd saved up.

Being on my own was challenging, but I loved knowing I was responsible for myself. I didn't have to depend on anyone for anything, and I'd never felt so free.

Freedom came with a price, though. I shoved my coat and bag into a locker in the back room of the bar and grill where I worked part time. Some event was happening at the fairgrounds, so we were expecting to be packed tonight. At least the tips ought to be good.

I was halfway through my shift when the hostess told me she'd just seated a single at one of my booths in the back. I grabbed a glass of water and a menu and headed that way.

"How's life treating you tonight?" I came up behind the man and set the water and menu on the table. Shoot, I thought I'd picked up a straw. I glanced back at the drink station, wondering if I'd dropped it on my way over.

"That depends."

My head snapped up. I hadn't heard his voice in

weeks, but I'd recognize it anywhere. What was Miles doing in Missoula? And what was he doing sitting at one of my tables in this hole-in-the-wall?

All the blood drained from my face and my cheeks went numb. "What... Why... How did you find me?"

"You look good, Kinley." His gaze traveled over my face. "Really, really good."

He looked good, too. Good enough to climb into his lap, bury my cheek against his chest and breathe in his fresh, outdoorsy scent.

"Excuse me, we'd like to get our check," a man at the table behind me said.

"What time do you get off?" Miles asked.

"Um, not until midnight." That was still three hours away, though I had no idea how I'd make it through the rest of my shift now that I'd seen Miles.

"Can we grab a cup of coffee or something when you're done?"

I think I nodded, but I couldn't be sure since my entire body had gone numb at the sound of his voice.

"Go take care of your tables. I'll wait right here until you're done."

"Um, we've got a line out the door. You'll have to order something or my boss will get pissed." Of all the things I could have said to him at the moment, I was worried about him taking up a table?

"Then bring me something. Anything you want." He didn't even look at the menu before he handed it back to me.

I nodded and tried to remember which table had asked for their check.

The next three hours passed in extreme slow motion. Finally, I closed out Miles's tab and sat down across from him.

"Thanks for talking to me, Kinley."

Hearing my name on his lips sent a shiver down my spine. "Whatever you have to say must be important if you drove all this way on a Friday night."

"It is." He reached into the front pocket of his jacket and pulled out an envelope. "I wanted to give you this."

"What is it?" I picked it up from where he'd set it between us, right next to the small container holding the fake sugar packets.

"Something I should have gotten for you before you left."

I eased the flap free and the picture I'd thought I'd lost forever slid out. "Where did you get this?"

He wrapped his hands around his mug and stared into his coffee. "I went back to Couer d'Alene on my way here."

"Miles, Couer d'Alene is the opposite direction from Mustang Mountain."

"So I took the long way." One of his shoulders lifted in a shrug as one side of his mouth curled into a half smile. "Doug was happy to part with it when I offered him enough cash for it."

I couldn't stop staring at the photograph.

"There's something else." He set a gift bag on the

table. "That picture's kind of small, and I don't want you to lose it again."

My fingers dug through the tissue paper to uncover a larger framed version of the same photograph. I didn't know what to say.

"Kinley, I owe you an apology." He reached out, his hand crossing the middle of the table. Without thinking about it, I slid my palm against his. "I'm sorry I made you feel like less than the incredible, smart, funny, capable, gorgeous woman that you are."

My heart stopped at the regret in his voice. "You were right to worry. I should have told you how much you meant to me. I'd been with Doug for five years and didn't feel a fraction toward him of what I felt for you. I never thought of you as my rebound guy. I thought of you as..."

His blue eyes drilled into me. "As what, baby?"

I tried to swallow, but my throat was too dry. "I thought of you as my forever guy."

"Is it too late for us?" His fingers gave mine a squeeze. Hope filled my chest. "I want to be your forever guy, Kinley. Want it more than anything. I want you by my side to pose for pictures with our kids. Want to make a home with you and build a beautiful life together."

I could barely force the words past the lump in my throat. "I want that too."

He held my gaze as he drew in a deep breath. "Will you come back to Mustang Mountain with me?"

The *yes* hovered on the tip of my tongue. I wanted

to, and I would. Just not yet. Not until I'd finished what I started. "Yes. When I'm done with my classes, I'd love to come back for good. Noelle told me I'd always be welcome to take a spot at the salon. I love you, Miles, love you more than anything. Will you wait for me?"

"Yes. If you'll let me get a place here so I can split my time between Missoula and Mustang Mountain. I don't want to be without you again."

Joy filled my heart. Everything was going to be okay. I'd found a man who wasn't threatened by a woman who wanted to follow her dreams. He loved me for who I was and who I wanted to be. I didn't have to change myself to make him feel bigger and better.

"Will you come back to my hotel with me tonight?" Heat edged its way into his eyes. "It's getting late, and I want to make sure you get a good night's sleep."

"You expect me to believe we'll be sleeping if I spend the night with you?" No chance. I'd been living without his touch for weeks.

"There might be some sleeping going on. After I let you have your way with me." He stood and leaned across the table to press a kiss to my lips. "Tomorrow we can start looking for an apartment."

"I'm paid up through next month with my roommates."

"Roommates?"

"Relax, they're two girls from my program, and they're going to love you. By the way, how did you know where to find me?"

He got up from his seat and pulled on his jacket. "Emma mentioned you were working at some restaurant near the fairgrounds, so I figured it couldn't be too hard."

I stood and gazed up at him. "How many places did you have to check?"

"I got lucky. Found you on stop number seventeen."

"You've been to sixteen other restaurants tonight?" I put my palm over his heart, eager to feel his pulse under my hand.

"One was more of a biker bar, but yeah." He put his hand over mine. "I would have kept looking until I found you, too."

I didn't doubt him. Not with the way his gaze burned into me. "You'll never have to go looking for me again because I don't plan on ever leaving you."

"Good. Now go grab your things so we can make up for lost time, baby."

My feet barely touched the ground as I hurried back to the break room to get my stuff. When I came down the hall to rejoin Miles, I stopped for a moment to take a good look at the man who owned my heart and soul. I'd missed that scruffy jaw, the way his shirts stretched tight across his pecs, and seeing his pulse beat at that spot at the base of his throat. I'd missed our lazy mornings in bed, our hikes through the peaceful woods, and our long talks in front of the fire.

He'd asked me if I'd go home with him, but I'd realized home wasn't a place. It was the way I felt deep down inside when we were together.

Wherever he was, that was where I wanted to be.

With him by my side, I'd always have a home.

"DAMMIT, RUBY!" I bite out as I pay for my to-go coffee.

"Oh, hush you. I'm three for three, and it's your turn!" She swats at me playfully with her bright red manicured nails, only I'm not playing.

"I don't want my picture and information plastered all over the town website!" I tell her, trying to make her understand I'm not playing around.

This is the fourth month in a row. She's done this and with Miles and Kinley getting together, I fear she won't ever stop.

"Come on, look at Jackson, Ford, and Miles over there. They're so happy. I just want that for you too and the rest of the Mustang Mountain Riders," she says, referring to the motorcycle club the guys and I are in.

I glance outside where the guys are standing around their trucks, waiting for me with their girls.

They are happy, but I don't know how much Ruby had to do with it. Ford and Luna have known each other since they were kids and Miles's girl literally jumped into his car out of nowhere. Jackson's with Miles's younger sister. So unless Ruby controls all things, she can't take credit for that. I won't fight with her. Not here like this, anyway.

"Take it down. You had your fun." I point at her to get her attention and leave the money for the coffee as I grab my to-go cup and head out the door.

At least I won't be the only single guy at the meeting today. Miles was able to grab Jonas and his brother Jensen too. I love these guys, but I wasn't thrilled to be doing wedding planning stuff.

"By the look on your face, I guess you saw you're Mr. April?" Luna cringes.

"You knew?" I growl. Ford gives me a look that says to knock it off. We may be brothers in arms, but he will protect his girl to the end.

"It just hit our emails while you were inside. I'm pretty sure we here in town are the last to be notified when it goes up," Emma says with a sad smile.

"Great," I mumble just as my phone rings.

I answer it and find my dispatcher at the mustang refuge on the other end of the line. She's a volunteer and works from home, so the sound of her baby crying fills the background as well.

"Asher, we just got a call that there's a horse, they think one of the wild mustangs, that was hit by a car. It's still alive." She goes on to give me the information and says she already has one of the volunteers on their way with the trailer for transport.

"There's a horse hit on the side of the road. I'm going to need some help," I tell the guys.

"We're in," Jensen says and nods to Jonas. Any reason to get out of this wedding stuff, I'm sure, and I can't blame them.

"Well, the girls can come with us and you two can go help too," Miles says and Jackson and Ford nod as we head out.

"Perfect, let's go," I say and we waste no time getting in my truck and following the directions my dispatcher texted me.

Not that we could miss it. There are no less than eight cars pulled over and people surrounding the horse, which is only stressing her out.

"Come on guys, do you want people crowding you when you're injured? Back the fuck up," I tell them, not giving a shit who I offend. I come from the rodeo circuit where everyone cusses worse than a cowboy with a nail through his boot. Most of these people are tourists, probably on their way to Glacier National Park. The locals know better and give wild animals plenty of room.

The guys and I get to work. They've helped me many times and jump right into it. Ford takes right to crowd control and gets everyone back across the street and away from the horse to give her and me some room.

Jackson, who has a way with animals, starts

working on calming her down. She seems mostly dazed and confused right now. Jensen jumps up to help guide my volunteer with the trailer in place as I assess her injuries with Jonas's help.

I've been a large animal vet for several years, but it never gets easier seeing them like this. I have to put my emotions aside and focus on the animal and what's best for her.

She's been hit by a car for sure and has a lot of open cuts. There's a lot of blood, but I don't think it's anything she can't recover from. But I need to get her back to the refuge where my clinic is and get her tranquilized and calm to really get a look. She's one of the wild mustangs and is afraid of people. I give her a mild sedative to help her relax enough to hopefully get her in the trailer.

Almost two hours later, we finally get her stable and back to the refuge where I'm able to look her over.

"How bad is it?" Jensen asks.

"I need an x-ray to check for internal injuries, but the external ones look worse than they are. There's a lot of blood, but as long as we stop any infection, the cuts aren't an issue. Just a few stitches," I tell him.

The guys stick around to help because moving a knocked-out horse around isn't easy. But we get all the tests done we need to. Thankfully, there's nothing going on internally other than some bruising, which is to be expected.

"She was lucky. I bet she ran into the street and the car tried to stop. It couldn't have been going too fast, or she'd have a lot more injuries," I tell them as we get her settled in her recovery stall and wait for one of the volunteers to get here to watch over her.

When she wakes up, there's a chance she might hurt herself because she won't know where she is and she'll go into defense mode and start to panic. We also want to make sure she doesn't have an adverse reaction to any of the medications we give her.

Watching her while she is out, she seems so peaceful, and it reminds me why I do what I do. I love helping these horses and I never regret the day that I made Mustang Mountain my home.

Once the volunteer comes to relieve me, I head back to my office to finally drink my now very cold cup of coffee. But, I get stopped on the way as I always seem to do.

"Asher, there's a woman here asking to speak to you," Donna, my receptionist, says.

We get people in all the time wanting to talk to the owner about this event or that media coverage. Charles is my PR guy and has taken over a lot of the event planning and social media too.

"Have her talk to Charles. I need to get the report going on that horse we just brought in," I tell her.

"No thank you. Charles isn't the father of my baby," a woman says with a voice I could never forget...

Want to read more about Miles and Kinley? Get a free

bonus scene here: https://www.matchofthemonth
books.com/Miles-Bonus

Did you miss the first two mountain men? Get their stories here...

January is for Jackson - https://www.matchofthe
monthbooks.com/January-Jackson

February is for Ford - https://www.matchofthe
monthbooks.com/February-Ford

MOUNTAIN MEN OF MUSTANG MOUNTAIN

Welcome to Mustang Mountain where love runs as wild as the free-spirited horses who roam the hillsides. Framed by rivers, lakes, and breathtaking mountains, it's also the place the Mountain Men of Mustang Mountain call home. They might be rugged and reclusive, but they'll risk their hearts for the curvy girls they love.

To learn more about the Mountain Men of Mustang Mountain, visit our website (https://www.matchofthemonthbooks.com/) join our newsletter here (http://subscribepage.io/MatchOfTheMonth) or follow our Patreon here (https://www.patreon.com/MatchOfTheMonth)

January is for Jackson - https://www.matchofthemonthbooks.com/January-Jackson

February is for Ford - https://www.matchofthe
monthbooks.com/February-Ford

March is for Miles - https://www.matchofthemon
thbooks.com/March-Miles

April is for Asher - https://www.matchofthemonth
books.com/April-Asher

May is for Mack - https://www.matchofthemonth
books.com/May-Mack

ACKNOWLEDGMENTS

A huge, heartfelt thanks goes to everyone who's supported us in our writing, especially our HUSSIES of Mountain Men of Mustang Mountain patrons:

Jackie Ziegler

To learn more about the Mountain Men of Mustang Mountain on Patreon, visit us here: https://www.patreon.com/MatchOfTheMonth

Mountain Men of Mustang Mountain Series

January is for Jackson

March is for Miles

May is for Mack

Whiskey Wars Series

Drinking Deep

Tasting Temptation

Sipping Seduction

Tying the Knot in Texas Series

The Cowboy Says I Do

Her Kind of Cowboy

Crazy About a Cowboy

Lovebird Café Series

Lemon Tarts & Stolen Hearts

Sweet Tea & Second Chances

Mud Pies & Family Ties

Hot Fudge & a Heartthrob

Holiday, Texas Series

All-American Cowboy

Cowboy Christmas Jubilee

Cowboy Charming

The Love Vixen Series

Getting Lucky in Love

Standalone Romances

All I Wanna Do Is You

Lonestar Riders MC Series*

One Night Series*

Matched with a Mountain Man Series**

Claimed by a Cowboy Series**

Summer Lovin' Series

Shared Series

March is for Miles - Mountain Men of Mustang Mountain

Curvy Cheeky Charmer* - The Galentine's Chronicles Series

Crushing on a Cowboy* - Everything's Bigger in Texas Series

January is for Jackson - Mountain Men of Mustang Mountain

One Night with a Diver* - Love on the Sunshine Coast Series

Hot Diggity Dogs* - Love at First Bark Series

Hot Drummer Summer* - Hot HEA Summer Series

One Night with a SEAL* - SEAL Team Romeo

Mustard Been You* - Sycamore Mountain Man of the Month Club

Hearts on Fire* - Hearts, Flames, and Hoses Series

Beaded by Midnight* - World's Biggest Party Series

Romancing the Quarterback* - Galentine's Getaway Series

Dating the Cowboy* - Matchmakers, Inc. Series

Kiss Off Countdown* - Midnight Kisses Series

Codename: Wolf* - Soldiers for Christmas Series

Room Twenty-Four - Club Sin Series

Dangerous Curves* - Curvy Soulmates Series

Trick or Tequila** - Halloween Steam Series

Single Dad Dilemma - Starlight Bay Series

* Features one of Mama Mae's boys as the hero

** Ties to one of Mama Mae's boys

ABOUT DYLANN CRUSH

USA Today bestselling author Dylann Crush writes contemporary romance with sizzle, sass, heart and humor. A true romantic, she loves her heroines spunky and her heroes super sexy. When she's not dreaming up steamy storylines, she can be found sipping a margarita and searching for the best Tex-Mex food in the Upper Midwest.

Dylann co-hosts Romance Happy Hour (https://www.romancehappyhour.com/) with live episodes every 2nd and 4th Thursday of each month and is the founder of Book Box Babe (https://www.BookBoxBabe.com) where readers can find hand-curated, romance novel themed subscription boxes, and specialty items.

Although she grew up in Texas, she currently lives in a suburb of Minneapolis/St. Paul with her unflappable husband, three energetic kids, a clumsy Great Dane, a lovable rescue mutt, a very chill cat, and a crazy kitten. She loves to connect with readers, other authors and fans of tequila.

You can find her at www.dylanncrush.com.

facebook.com/dylanncrush

instagram.com/dylanncrush

pinterest.com/dylanncrush

bookbub.com/authors/dylann-crush

goodreads.com/DylannCrush

tiktok.com/@dylanncrush

ABOUT EVE LONDON

When Eve London was a girl she wanted to be a trapeze artist. Instead, she grew up to be like most women–a juggler–trying to keep bunches of balls in the air.

Now she spends her days writing about the kind of men she likes – sexy, shameless, and just a little bit sarcastic.

www.EveLondonAuthor.com

facebook.com/evelondonauthor

instagram.com/evelondonbooks

bookbub.com/authors/eve-london

patreon.com/EveLondon